MADAGASCAR™

BORN TO BE WILD

By Erica David

DreamWorks
ANIMATION SKG

Scholastic Inc.

New York   Toronto   London   Auckland   Sydney
Mexico City   New Delhi   Hong Kong   Buenos Aires

ISBN: 0-439-69625-9

Madagascar TM & © 2005 DreamWorks Animation L.L.C.

Published by Scholastic Inc.
SCHOLASTIC and associated logos are trademarks and/or registered trademarks of Scholastic Inc.

12 11 10 9 8 7 6 5 4 3 2 1   5 6 7 8 9/0

Printed in the U.S.A.
First printing, May 2005

Marty the zebra ran through the lush, green jungle. It was beautiful. Wide open spaces . . . the wind in his mane . . . what more could a zebra want?

Suddenly a loud voice startled Marty. It was Alex the lion wishing him a happy birthday. Marty looked around. He wasn't in the wild. He was home — at the zoo. He'd just been staring at his mural and daydreaming.

"Every year it's the same old thing," Marty sighed. "I'm bored."
Alex suggested that he try a new routine in his zoo act, and find a way to keep it fresh.

When the zoo opened, people gathered around Marty's pen. He decided to try some new moves. He moonwalked. He made armpit noises.

Marty even pretended to be a fountain. He sprayed the crowd with water.

Even though Marty had changed his act, he still felt restless. The only excitement was when some penguins suddenly popped up in his enclosure.

"What are you doing?" Marty asked.
"We're escaping to the wild," said a penguin.
"The wild? You can really go there? I thought it was just a dream," said Marty.

That night Marty blew out the candle on his cake.

"What did you wish for?" asked Gloria the hippo.

"I wished I could go to the wild!" Marty said.

"That's crazy!" cried Melman the giraffe. "It's scary and full of germs!"

"Marty, you're my best friend," said Alex. "Are you going to go to the wild and leave all your friends behind?"
Later that night, Marty had an idea. He would explore the city, take a train to the wild, and be back in the morning.

13

Back at the zoo, Marty's friends discovered that he was missing.
"What do we do?" cried Melman.

"We have to go after him," said Alex.
"If the zoo finds out he's gone, he'll be in
trouble!" Gloria exclaimed.
The three friends had only one choice —
break out of the zoo and find Marty!

Alex, Gloria, and Melman ventured into the
subway to search for their missing friend.
The people on the subway were scared to
see a lion, a hippo, and a giraffe riding right
beside them. The zoo friends didn't notice.
They were too busy looking for Marty.

Alex, Gloria, and Melman found Marty at the train station. Unfortunately, so did the police.

Alex tried to explain to the people so they wouldn't get in trouble, but it was no use. They were all captured — even the penguins!

The next day the four friends were packed into crates and put on a ship heading for Africa.

"Nice going, Marty," snarled Alex.

"It's not my fault," Marty said.

"Yes it is. We had a good life at the zoo," Alex told him. "People took care of us. Now they're sending us away because you had to go to the wild."

The boat carrying the animals made a sudden
turn. The ropes holding the crates snapped.
Marty and his friends fell overboard!
Alex, Gloria, and Melman washed up on the
shore of an island.

No one could find Marty.
"Where could he be?" Alex wondered.
Just then, Marty surfed in on the backs of
two dolphins.

Now everyone was together. But where were they?

"Wide open enclosures," noted Melman. "Must be the zoo in San Diego."

But they weren't in San Diego at all. They were in the wild. Marty was the only one who was happy about that. He thought the wild was crack-a-lackin'.

"If you hadn't wished to go to the wild this never would have happened!" Alex roared. He drew a line in the sand and pointed at Marty.

"From now on you stay on *that* side of the island! *This* side is for those of us who love New York and want to go home," said Alex.

Alex built a statue to signal a rescue boat. But Melman accidentally set it on fire and it burned to the ground.

Marty kept to his side of the island. He fished and made a campfire and even built a house. Gloria and Melman saw how much fun Marty was having. They decided to join him on his side of the island — the fun side.

Alex felt left out. He missed his friends.
"I'm sorry I blamed you," Alex apologized to
Marty. "Do you think I can come to the fun
side, too?"
"Sure," Marty said. "There's always room for
one more."

That night the four friends sat by the fire,
eating seaweed on a stick.
It wasn't very tasty, but it was fun to be
together again.

The next day Alex saw something that he wanted to show Marty.

"Look at this view!" Marty cried. "It's just like my mural at the zoo!"

Gloria, Alex, and Melman looked out at the view. It *was* beautiful. Maybe they could get used to the wild after all.